First edition for the United States, Canada,
Australia and the Philippines published 1988
by Barron's Educational Series, Inc.

First published 1987 by Walker Books, Ltd., London, England

Copyright © 1987 Colin West

All inquiries should be addressed to:
Barron's Educational Series, Inc.
250 Wireless Boulevard, Hauppauge, NY 11788

Library of Congress Catalog Card No. 87-16780
International Standard Book No. 0-8120-5885-2

Library of Congress Cataloging-in-Publication Data
West, Colin.
One little elephant.
Summary: As an elephant is joined by others, one at a time
the reader may count from one to ten.
[1. Elephant—Fiction. 2. Counting]   I. Title.
PZ7.W517440n   1988   [E]   87-16780

ISBN 0-8120-5885-2

Printed in Hong Kong by Dai Nippon (H.K.) Ltd.
789   9685   987654321

One Little Elephant

Colin West

BARRON'S
New York · Toronto · Sydney

One little elephant
Wondering what to do,

Once there was an elephant,
And then there were . . .

Two little elephants
Surfing on the sea,

Once there were two elephants,
And then there were . . .

Three little elephants
Singing at my door,

Once there were three elephants,
And then there were . . .

Four little elephants
Learning how to jive,

Once there were four elephants,
And then there were . . .

Five little elephants
Doing funny tricks,

Once there were five elephants,
And then there were . . .

Six little elephants
Think the beach is heaven,

Once there were six elephants,
And then there were . . .

Seven little elephants
Trying hard to skate,

Once there were seven elephants,
And then there were . . .

8

Eight little elephants
Skipping in a line,

Once there were eight elephants,
And then there were . . .

Nine little elephants
Snoozing now and then,

Once there were nine elephants
And then there were . . .

Ten little elephants
Playing in the rain,

Once there were ten elephants,
Let's count them all again . . .

Ten little elephants
Have had a lot of fun . . .

Once there were ten elephants,
But now their tale is done!